THE TICKLE TREE

THE TICKLE TREE

by
Fran Manushkin

Illustrated by
Yuri Salzman

CLARION BOOKS
TICKNOR & FIELDS : A HOUGHTON MIFFLIN COMPANY
NEW YORK

To my good friend
Jerry Boyke
—F.M.

To my wife
Marianna
—Y.S.

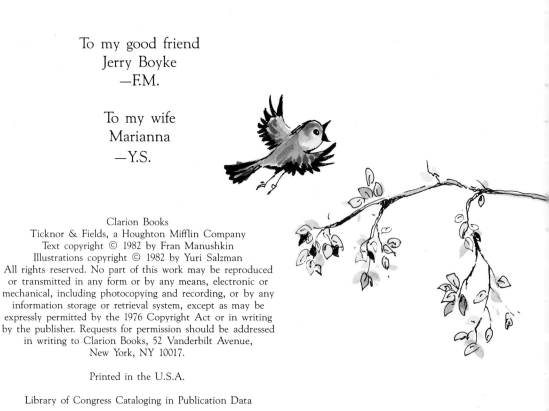

Clarion Books
Ticknor & Fields, a Houghton Mifflin Company
Text copyright © 1982 by Fran Manushkin
Illustrations copyright © 1982 by Yuri Salzman

Printed in the U.S.A.

Library of Congress Cataloging in Publication Data

Manushkin, Fran. The tickle tree.
Summary: In his search for the best tickle
in the world, a squirrel enlists the help of
a cat, a rooster, some chicks, a goat, a horse,
a camel, and finally, a palm tree.
[1.Animals—Fiction] I.Salzman, Yuri, ill.
II. Title
PZ7.M3195Ti   [E]   81-12315
ISBN 0-89919-077-4   AACR2

Once there was a squirrel
who loved being tickled.
Oh, how he loved being tickled!

One day the squirrel met a cat.
"Please tickle me,"
said the squirrel.

So the cat crept up to the squirrel
and tickled him with his whiskers.
"Ha!" laughed the squirrel.
"I liked that. But I want
a bigger tickle."

The squirrel met a rooster.
"Tickle me!" said the squirrel.
So the rooster tickled the squirrel
with his bushy tail.

"Ho Ho!" laughed the squirrel.
"That was pretty good! But I want
a BIGGER tickle."

"Meet my chicks," said the rooster.
"Hello," said the squirrel.
"Will you please tickle me?"

The chicks giggled
and leaped onto the squirrel.
They tickled him and tickled him
and tickled him.
"Hee—hee—hee!" laughed the squirrel.
"That was a really fine tickle.
But I want a GREAT tickle."

The squirrel wandered along
until he came to a wheat field.
"Maybe the wheat
can tickle me," he thought.

The squirrel jumped into the wheat
and made it tickle him all over.
"Oh, that feels good!"
said the squirrel.
"But it still isn't tickly enough."

Suddenly, at the edge of the field,
the squirrel saw an amazing thing.
"It's a Tickle Tree!" he shouted.
"How I'd love to be tickled
by a Tickle Tree!"

Just then a goat trotted by.
"Hello, Goat," called the squirrel,
"I want to reach the top of that tree.
 May I stand on your back?"
"Sure," said the goat.

The squirrel hopped onto
the goat's back.
But he couldn't reach
the Tickle Tree.

Then a horse galloped by.
"Hello, Horse," said the squirrel.
"May I stand on your back?"
"Why not?" said the horse.

So the squirrel
stood on the horse's back.
But he still couldn't reach
the Tickle Tree.

"Try me," said a passing camel.
"Thank you!" said the squirrel.
He leaped onto the camel,
but he still couldn't reach
the Tickle Tree.

"What am I going to do?" said the squirrel.

"Try this," said the goat.
    He stood on the horse,
    and the squirrel stood
    on the goat.
    But the squirrel still couldn't reach
    that Tickle Tree.

"I have a better idea,"
said the squirrel.
"I'll stand on Goat,
and Goat can stand on Horse,
and Horse can stand on Camel."
So they did.
And the squirrel finally
reached the Tickle Tree.

"Tickle me!" he told the tree.
 And it did.
 It tickled him here...
 and it tickled him there.
"Hooooo, hoooooo!" laughed the squirrel.
"HOOOOO, HOOOOOO," laughed
 the goat, and the horse,
 and the camel.

They laughed so hard
that the Tickle Tree started to sway.
It swayed and swayed,
until—SWOOOSH!—
the squirrel
and his friends
all tumbled down.

"Thank you all," said the squirrel.
"That was a perfect tickle."
"Now I'm ready to go to sleep."

"So are we," said the goat and the horse
and the camel.

So they all snuggled up
together
and fell asleep
under the friendly
Tickle Tree.

Good Night.

ST. THOMAS LUTHERAN SCHOOL
23801 KELLY ROAD
EAST DETROIT, MICHIGAN 48021